1914

Rebecca
TO THE RESCUE

BY JACQUELINE DEMBAR GREENE

ILLUSTRATIONS ROBERT HUNT

VIGNETTES SUSAN MCALILEY

★ AmericanGirl®

THE AMERICAN GIRLS

1764

KAYA, an adventurous Nez Perce girl whose deep love for horses and respect for nature nourish her spirit

1774

FELICITY, a spunky, spritely colonial girl, full of energy and independence

1824

JOSEFINA, a Hispanic girl whose heart and hopes are as big as the New Mexico sky

1854

KIRSTEN, a pioneer girl of strength and spirit who settles on the frontier

1864

ADDY, a courageous girl determined to be free in the midst of the Civil War

1904

SAMANTHA, a bright Victorian beauty, an orphan raised by her wealthy grandmother

1914

REBECCA, a lively girl with dramatic flair growing up in New York City

1934

KIT, a clever, resourceful girl facing the Great Depression with spirit and determination

1944

MOLLY, who schemes and dreams on the home front during World War Two

1974

JULIE, a fun-loving girl from San Francisco who faces big changes—and creates a few of her own

Published by American Girl Publishing, Inc.
Copyright © 2009 by American Girl, LLC

Questions or comments? Call 1-800-845-0005, visit **americangirl.com**,
or write to Customer Service, American Girl, 8400 Fairway Place,
Middleton, WI 53562-0497.

Printed in China
10 11 12 13 14 15 16 LEO 11 10 9 8 7 6 5 4

All American Girl marks, Rebecca™, Rebecca Rubin™, and Ana™
are trademarks of American Girl, LLC.

PICTURE CREDITS
The following individuals and organizations have generously
given permission to reprint images contained in "Looking Back":
pp. 64–65—Christopher Cardozo Inc. (beach scene); Coney Island Museum
(girls lying on sand); Courtesy of The Brooklyn Historical Society (Seeing Coney Island);
pp. 66–67—courtesy of Howard Brookstein (Steeplechase Park ticket); Dreamland Press
(Steeplechase Park aerial view); pp. 68–69—Library of Congress (Victorian girls);
Bettmann/Corbis (women riding carousel)

Library of Congress Cataloging-in-Publication Data

Greene, Jacqueline Dembar.
Rebecca to the rescue / by Jacqueline Dembar Greene ;
illustrations, Robert Hunt ; vignettes, Susan McAliley.
p. cm.
Summary: While celebrating her brother's Bar Mitzvah on Coney Island,
nine-year-old Rebecca Rubin disobeys by going off on her own, leaving her cousin Ana,
a recent immigrant, alone.
ISBN 978-1-59369-528-6 (pbk.) — ISBN 978-1-59369-529-3 (hardcover)
1. Jews—New York (State)—New York—Juvenile fiction. [1. Jews—United States—Fiction.
2. Amusement parks—Fiction. 3. Coney Island (New York, N.Y.)—Fiction.
4. Bar mitzvah—Fiction. 5. Family life—New York (State)—New York—Fiction.
6. New York (N.Y.)—History—20th century—Fiction.]
I. Hunt, Robert, 1952–, ill. II. McAliley, Susan, ill. III. Title.
PZ7.G834Rem 2009   [Fic]—dc22   2009017759

TO MONTY, LAURIE, MARTHA, AND JANE,
WHO CHEERED ME ON EVEN WHEN
THE RIDE GOT BUMPY

Rebecca's parents and grandparents came to America before Rebecca was born, along with millions of other Jewish immigrants from different parts of the world. These immigrants brought with them many different traditions and ways of being Jewish. Practices varied widely between families, and differences among Jewish families were just as common in Rebecca's time as they are today. Rebecca's stories show the way one Jewish family could have lived in 1914 and 1915.

Rebecca's grandparents spoke mostly *Yiddish*, a language that was common among Jews from Eastern Europe. For help in pronouncing or understanding the foreign words in this book, look in the glossary on page 70.

TABLE OF CONTENTS

REBECCA'S FAMILY AND FRIENDS

CHAPTER ONE
A BAR MITZVAH CELEBRATION   1

CHAPTER TWO
STEEPLECHASE—THE FUNNY PLACE   16

CHAPTER THREE
THRILLS, CHILLS, AND SKILLS   29

CHAPTER FOUR
STRIKING OUT ALONE   39

CHAPTER FIVE
REACHING NEW HEIGHTS   47

LOOKING BACK   63

GLOSSARY   70

A SNEAK PEEK AT *CHANGES FOR REBECCA*   71

REBECCA'S FAMILY

PAPA
Rebecca's father, an understanding man who owns a small shoe store

MAMA
Rebecca's mother, who keeps a good Jewish home—and a good sense of humor

REBECCA
A lively girl with dramatic flair, growing up in New York City

SADIE AND SOPHIE
Rebecca's twin sisters, who like to remind Rebecca that they are fourteen

BENNY AND VICTOR
Rebecca's brothers, who are six and thirteen

GRANDPA
*Rebecca's grandfather,
an immigrant from
Russia who carries on
the Jewish traditions*

BUBBIE
*Rebecca's grandmother,
an immigrant from
Russia who is feisty
and outspoken*

ANA
*Rebecca's cousin, an
immigrant from Russia
who is learning to be
an American*

MAX
*Mama's cousin, who
leads the exciting life
of an actor*

LILY
*A movie star who doesn't
shy away from new roles,
onscreen and in life*

A BAR MITZVAH
CELEBRATION

"I can't believe you closed the shoe store today, Papa," said Rebecca. "Saturday is your busiest day of the week."

Papa straightened his tie. "It's not every day that your son becomes a *Bar Mitzvah*," he said with a note of pride. Rebecca's brother Victor was thirteen now, the age when Jewish boys were considered full members of the congregation, and today he would join the men in prayer.

Grandpa had been teaching Victor to read the Hebrew prayers since he was eight years old. Grandpa could be a demanding tutor, and he became impatient when Victor made the tiniest mistake. He insisted Victor recite over and over

1

again until each line was perfect. Finally Grandpa had decided that Victor was ready.

Rebecca knew it was an important day for her brother. Still, she was tired of everyone making a fuss over him. Mama let him stay up late to do his homework. Papa brought him to the family's shoe store and let him choose a fancy pair of leather oxfords. And Grandpa spent every extra minute studying with Victor. All the attention had made Victor quite bossy. He yelled at little brother Benny if he made any noise while Victor was studying. He ordered Rebecca and her sisters around when he wanted something to eat or drink. Rebecca tried to stay out of Victor's way, but it was hard in such a small apartment.

Rebecca crept up to her parents' closed bedroom door. Inside, she could hear Victor and Grandpa going over the passage Victor would read aloud from the Torah, the ancient scroll that contained the first five books of Jewish Scripture.

Torah

Rebecca's twin sisters, Sadie and Sophie, quietly joined her at the door. All three strained to hear Victor practicing for the last time.

He began chanting the Hebrew words in a mellow tone, when suddenly a high-pitched sound squeaked out of his throat. Her brother's voice had cracked! It sounded as if little Benny had spoken for his older brother. Rebecca nearly burst out laughing. She and the twins stifled their giggles and hurried away from the door.

"I think Victor has a bigger problem than reading the Hebrew words without a mistake," Rebecca said. The girls dissolved into gales of laughter, just as Victor came into the kitchen.

"What's so funny?" he asked, stretching importantly in his new suit.

"You are," Sadie laughed. "You may be a man today, but your voice doesn't seem to know it!"

Victor narrowed his eyes. "Stop trying to make me nervous," he barked. "You're just plain jealous."

"That's enough," Mama interrupted, patting Victor soothingly on his back. "This is a day to celebrate, not to fight." She shooed everyone toward the door, and the family filed out, with Papa and Grandpa leading the parade.

People dressed in their best clothes strolled along the sidewalk and called out, "Good *Shabbos!*" Rebecca and her family gaily returned the wish for a pleasant Sabbath as they walked to the synagogue on Eldridge Street.

"Doesn't your brother look grown-up in his suit?" Mama asked, but only Benny nodded enthusiastically. "I can't believe he's out of short pants already," Mama sighed. Rebecca and the twins looked at each other and rolled their eyes. *It's Victor this, and Victor that,* Rebecca thought with exasperation. *Victor, Victor, Victor!*

"I'd rather be playing baseball," Victor muttered, but Rebecca thought he was just bluffing. Who wouldn't love being the center of so much attention?

"You couldn't play very well in *that* outfit," Rebecca scoffed.

"I could play in anything," Victor boasted.

"Oh, really? Then so could I!" said Rebecca sarcastically, taunting her brother.

Victor smirked. "Right, I can just see you running around the bases in a dress! You couldn't play baseball if you wore a Yankees uniform."

Rebecca swatted Victor on the arm, but he just strode off and caught up with Papa and Grandpa.

A friend of Grandpa's fell into step behind them, his long beard hanging down onto his shirt.

"*Mazel tov!*" he congratulated Victor. "I see from the trousers that today you are a man, eh?"

"First he will pray with the men," Grandpa said. "If he doesn't make a mistake, then you can give him a 'mazel tov.' But not yet!"

Victor squirmed and tugged at his jacket. Rebecca knew he was nervous. It wouldn't be easy to stand before the entire congregation and chant the Hebrew passage alone. Victor had practiced hard the past few months, but sometimes he still made mistakes. And what if his voice cracked?

"So, after the prayers, a nice celebration, eh?" persisted the man.

"Nothing fancy," Papa said. "Tomorrow we'll have a family picnic." Rebecca didn't know where the picnic would be, since Papa wanted it to be a surprise. Mama and Bubbie had refused to reveal the secret. Rebecca hoped it was someplace she'd never been before, like Central Park.

"I don't see why everyone is making such a fuss about a Bar Mitzvah," Sadie complained. "And why should boys be the only ones who read from the Torah? If Grandpa had taught me Hebrew, I could do it, too." The springy curl at her forehead bounced as she walked.

"Me, too," Rebecca chimed in. "I'm much better at memorizing than Victor."

"Boys get to do everything," Sadie grumbled, and Sophie nodded in agreement.

"Enough with the *kvetching*," Mama scolded. She didn't like complaints.

"To be a good Jewish wife and mother, you girls still have plenty to learn," said Bubbie. "You must keep the house *kosher* and observe the Sabbath every week. The men will do the Torah reading."

Yet Rebecca couldn't help thinking that boys did get to do a lot more than girls, and not only studying Hebrew. Papa let Victor go off to places that even his older sisters weren't allowed to visit alone. And in school, the teachers almost always chose boys to be class monitors or to run errands.

Still, Rebecca had to admit that her brother had worked hard for this special moment. On top of his regular schoolwork each day, Victor had done all the lessons that Grandpa gave him.

As Rebecca approached the wide steps of the synagogue, she saw her cousin Ana waiting with her family. Rebecca started to shout hello, but in the nick of time, she held her tongue and just waved. She knew Mama would scold if she raised her voice in front of the synagogue, even for a greeting.

Cousins Josef and Michael slapped Victor on the shoulder. "Don't worry," Josef said. "We both read from Torah when we turned thirteen back in Russia. Is not so hard!"

"Victor is looking like grown-up," Ana remarked to Rebecca.

"Whatever you do, don't tell him," Rebecca replied. "His head is already too big."

Ana looked critically at Victor. "Head is not too big," she said. "Maybe just ears."

Rebecca smiled fondly. Ana had learned English well since her family had arrived in America, but she still made some funny mistakes.

As the family opened the heavy wooden doors of the synagogue, cousin Max came around the corner with a young woman on his arm. They didn't have to get any closer for Rebecca to know who it was.

"That's Lillian Armstrong," she whispered to Ana.

"The actress?" Ana gasped. "I can't believe a real actress is coming to your brother's Bar Mitzvah!"

"Shhh!" said Rebecca. "Don't let Bubbie hear. She doesn't think acting is respectable, especially for a lady."

Max introduced Lily to the family. "This is Lillian Aronovich," he said. Rebecca raised her eyebrows in surprise. Lily must have changed her name from Aronovich to Armstrong so that it would sound more American, just as Max had changed his name from Moyshe Shereshevsky to Max Shepard. Bubbie hadn't approved of that, either.

Rebecca was delighted to see that Max and Lily were keeping company. Rebecca wanted to give Lily a hug, but then she would have to explain where she had met Lily before—at the movie studio. The family might decide they didn't approve of Lily, just because she was an actress. Rebecca greeted Lily with a formal handshake, but she broke into a smile when Lily secretly winked at her.

"So, where you two meet each other?" Grandpa asked Max.

"Shouldn't we go in," Rebecca interrupted, "so Victor can get settled?" She didn't want Max to have to explain that he and Lily were working together in a movie. "What a pretty dress, Miss Aronovich," she said quickly.

Lily wore a lacy white summer dress and had covered her hair with a large straw hat. No one would ever guess that beneath the hat, her hair was cropped in a shocking bob. There wasn't a trace of makeup on Lily's face. Rebecca guessed that Lily wanted to make a good impression on the family. It seemed to be working. Mama smiled warmly at Max, and Bubbie allowed Lily to take her arm and escort her inside.

"So, your family comes from Russia?" Bubbie asked.

"They come from Kiev in the Ukraine," said Lily. Bubbie patted Lily's hand approvingly.

In the synagogue, Papa made sure that Victor knew the proper way to wear the long prayer shawl. He beamed as Victor draped it around his shoulders, but Rebecca noticed that Victor's hands were trembling.

prayer shawl

Rebecca headed toward the balcony where the women sat, overlooking the men at prayer. As she

9

 started up the stairs, she traced her finger around the bold Star of David carved in the newel post at the foot of the staircase. Behind her, Mama tugged Benny as he tried to pull away. "I want to go with Papa," Benny whined.

"Not until you start learning Hebrew," Mama told him. "And learn to sit still." Benny pouted, and he stomped his feet all the way up the stairs.

As they settled into the front row for the best view, Rebecca gazed at the two enormous stained-glass windows that glowed at each end of the cavernous room. Each round frame held twelve colorful rosettes, one for each of the twelve tribes of Israel. Rebecca felt a sense of peace enveloping her as a hush fell over the congregation.

"Is beautiful here," Ana whispered. "So bright and lovely, and so quiet. Not like our tenement, where everything is dark, and there is noise every minute."

The cantor began to sing a welcoming song, and Rebecca let the sound wash over her. Mama gave Benny a stern look until he stopped swinging his legs. She handed him a prayer book, which he promptly opened, holding the book upside down.

*Rebecca felt a sense of peace enveloping her as a
hush fell over the congregation.*

11

After the opening prayers, the rabbi took the Torah from its special cabinet. The parchment scroll was draped in a velvet covering embroidered in thick gold thread. Setting the cover aside, the rabbi unfurled the parchment scroll until he found the passage for the day.

"Bubbie embroidered the Torah cover," Rebecca whispered in Lily's ear. It was an honor to be asked by the rabbi to work on such a project, and Rebecca was sure Lily would remember to compliment Bubbie on her needlework skills.

With a firm grip, Papa lifted the Torah by the two bottom handles, raising it high in the air while the rabbi intoned in a deep voice, "This is the Torah that Moses placed before the people of Israel." Papa carefully laid the hand-lettered scroll on a high table as the rabbi called Victor by his Hebrew name.

Victor looked pale as he ascended the platform that stood near the front of the synagogue, and Rebecca felt a sympathetic flutter in her own stomach. The platform was like a stage, and today Victor was in the spotlight, but he wasn't acting. This was real.

Victor touched the fringe of his prayer shawl to the Torah and chanted a prayer in a shaky voice.

Then he read the Hebrew words, keeping his place with a long silver pointer. His voice grew stronger and his melodic chanting rose up, filling the synagogue. When he had finished, the rabbi led the handshakes. Victor's voice hadn't cracked once, and Rebecca breathed a sigh of relief for her brother.

Papa and Grandpa swelled with pride. Mama dabbed at her eyes with a handkerchief as the women in the balcony leaned forward and offered their good wishes. Rebecca's heart beat faster. Her brother had joined the men now. He was still her annoying brother, but in her eyes, he had grown up considerably.

Benny raced down the stairs as soon as the service ended. He hugged Victor's legs and squealed, "Mazel tov!"

Juice, coffee, and pastries were set out in a side room, and Victor was ushered to the front of the line. He filled a plate and basked in congratulations.

"Such a *mensch!*" said a big woman in a flouncy dress as she pinched Victor's cheek. A red mark glowed where her fingers had squeezed.

Aunt Fannie kissed Victor and began talking excitedly in Yiddish.

"Mama, speak English!" Ana urged her. "If you are speaking always Yiddish, how you will learn English like me?"

Aunt Fannie looked embarrassed. "I think I am speaking English," she explained, "but out from my mouth is coming Yiddish!" Everyone laughed sympathetically.

Max slapped Victor on the back. "You really hit a home run today," he said. "What do you say we go watch the Yankees hit a few next week?"

"Do you really mean it?" Victor asked. "I've been wanting to go to a ball game forever!" He glanced shyly at Lily. "Maybe Miss Aronovich can come, too."

Lily looked rather shocked, and Rebecca wondered if she was acting. "Oh, no," Lily protested. "A ballpark is no place for a lady. Those games are for men!" Bubbie nodded her agreement.

Lily took Max's arm. "It was so nice to meet you all," she said as they turned to go. "Congratulations, young man." She gave Victor a little peck on the cheek, and he blushed a deep crimson.

"Before you hurry off," Papa said to Max, "are you free tomorrow? We've got a holiday planned, and you're both welcome to join us." Papa leaned toward Max and lowered his voice mysteriously. "You'll be sorry if you miss this little trip."

"Where are we going, Papa?" Benny asked, pulling at his father's sleeve. "Let's go to the park!"

"That's exactly what I have planned," Papa said. "A day at the park." He broke into a grin. "Steeplechase Park."

"At Coney Island?" Victor exclaimed. "Thanks, Pop!"

Rebecca's friends had told her about the splashing waves and wild rides at Coney Island. It sounded like a wonderland, with strange and delightful things to see and do. She had tried to imagine what it was like. Tomorrow, she would find out.

Max caught her eye and leaned closer. "Just the place for you, my little starlet," he said softly. "You're going to be dazzled!"

C H A P T E R
T W O
—

STEEPLECHASE— THE FUNNY PLACE

The steamship to Coney Island glided toward the pier, while seagulls soared and wheeled overhead.

"What lucky birds," Rebecca said. "They get to come to Coney Island every day."

The gangplank was lowered, and Ana, Rebecca, and their familes joined the crowd of people streaming down the long pier.

"What?" Bubbie grumbled. "Everybody in New York is coming here with us?" She jostled her way along, elbowing anyone who tried to hem her in.

"Look," Rebecca cried. "There's the Funny Face!" She had seen it before on posters advertising

Steeplechase Park. In the distance, a huge
Funny Face sign loomed over the
entrance to the amusement park, its
gigantic grin both silly and challenging.

All around, barkers shouted to the crowd. "Step
right up, ladies and gentlemen! Come and see the
most amazing creatures that have ever called
themselves human!" Rebecca saw freakish pictures
painted on a large canvas sign. There was a
bearded lady, a man with webbed feet, and a
"rubber boy" whose bones could bend in half. As
she gaped at them, two of the tiniest people Rebecca
had ever seen strolled by, pushing a Chihuahua in a
baby carriage. When they got to a turnstile, they
walked right under it without even bending over.
Rebecca couldn't help staring at the odd family.

"Follow me to the beach," Papa said. "First we'll
eat, and when the picnic baskets are empty, we'll
head inside."

Rebecca and Ana skipped along hand in hand.
The fresh salty breeze mixed with the smells of
clams, fish, and potatoes frying at sidewalk stands.

"Steeplechase, Steeplechase, the man with the
funny face," Rebecca sang. She had heard her friends

at school singing the rhyme as they jumped rope, and now she had seen the real Funny Face for herself.

"Hot dogs here!" yelled a man pulling the long sausages from a steamer. "Get yer Coney Island Red Hots for just a nickel!"

A sea of people swarmed across the beach, and Rebecca's family came to a halt, wondering where they could find space to eat their lunch. Max pointed to the shade of a wooden pier, and the family trooped toward it, their feet sinking into the loose sand with every step.

Two young women dressed in limp wool bathing outfits dashed past them, running toward the splashing surf. Rebecca watched longingly as they hung on to a thick rope that stretched over the waves, laughing and frolicking in the water while holding on for dear life.

Bubbie looked at the bathers romping on the beach. "For shame," she said crossly. "Look at how people behave here—and such clothes! Where are the manners?"

"I want to go in the ocean!" Benny announced. He began pulling off his shoes and stockings.

"You need a bathing suit to go in," Papa told him. "What will you wear today if your clothes get all wet?"

"I'll take them off and *then* go bathing!" Benny declared.

Sadie and Sophie burst out laughing. "Gosh, Benny," Sophie chided, "you can't run around without any clothes—even at Coney Island!" She helped Mama and Aunt Fannie arrange the food on a thin blanket they had spread on the sand.

Josef swiped a pickle and took a crunching bite. "Back there is place to rent bathing suits," he said casually. "We could all go in ocean."

Uncle Jacob frowned. "It costs twenty-five cents for one of those crazy outfits. Just for getting wet in!" Josef dropped his head and munched his pickle without another word.

Rebecca did a quick tally. There were eight children and eight adults. If everyone rented a bathing outfit, it would cost four whole dollars! Then she perked up.

"Well, wading is free," she remarked, slipping

19

off her shoes and stockings. "Come on, Benny, let's cool off." Benny grabbed her hand, and Rebecca led him across the sand.

"Don't let go of him!" Mama called. But she didn't have to worry, for all the youngsters were now removing their shoes and stockings and heading toward the water's edge. Benny would have lots of hands holding on to him.

"It's *meshugah!*" Bubbie sputtered. "Everyone has gone crazy!"

The girls held their skirts up to their knees, trying not to get their clothes wet, and the boys rolled up their trousers and jumped over the waves as they splashed ashore. Benny squealed with delight, stamping his feet and slapping his hands against the water.

The sun beat down hotter. "That's enough for me," Rebecca said after a while. "My head is getting too hot and my feet are getting too cold."

"And I'm starving," Victor said. They trooped back to the blanket.

Lily was sitting primly beside Bubbie, discussing embroidery. Today her hat was held on with a loose scarf that tied under her chin and hid her cropped hair. Rebecca noticed that Lily's scarf had loosened in the sea breeze.

Bubbie musn't see Lily's hair bob, Rebecca worried. *What will she think?* Rebecca caught Lily's eye and gestured at her own hair until Lily understood her silent message. Lily pulled her scarf tighter until her short hair was safely covered again.

"Eat, eat!" Aunt Fannie urged, and before long, the lunch had disappeared and the baskets and blankets were packed up. Rebecca brushed sand from between her toes and wiggled back into her stockings. Sadie and Sophie pulled up their stockings and replaced their shoes.

"I can't believe I am dressing in front of strangers," Sophie said, blushing as men with bare shoulders skipped merrily along the sand in the company of women in open-necked bathing outfits.

"At least you are *dressed*," Bubbie huffed. "Naked feet is bad enough!"

At the entrance to Steeplechase Park, Papa bought combination tickets for the rides. The family entered an enormous glass pavilion. Rebecca gawked at the mirrored carousel in the center, with three tiers of carved, painted animals circling around. A glittering canopy of lights and mirrors covered the entire carousel, and a band organ pumped out lively music. Bells, cymbals, and drums reverberated throughout the pavilion and made Rebecca feel like dancing.

Papa handed the tickets to Victor. Each ticket was good for one turn on the most popular rides. "You're in charge of keeping all the young people together," he said. "And make sure the girls don't ride anything too dangerous."

Victor's voice swelled with confidence. "I'll watch out for everyone," he assured his father, holding the tickets firmly.

Sadie sniffed. "I don't need to be looked after by my little brother," she declared.

Grandpa gestured toward the crush of people. "A young lady shouldn't be on her own in this place."

"And those rides," Bubbie fretted. Clattering rides whizzed overhead. "People acting like monkeys, swinging through the air. You shouldn't step foot on such dangerous contraptions!"

Papa took Bubbie's elbow and steered her away. "We'll leave the wild amusements to the youngsters while we take a walk. I hear there's a beautiful rose garden. We'll all meet back here at four o'clock," he said, handing Victor his pocket watch. Bubbie's face turned red with worry, but she let Papa steer her off.

Benny tugged Mama's arm, pulling toward the bright carousel. "I want to ride a horse!" he cried. "Where's *my* ticket?"

Mama grasped his hand. "You're staying with me," she said flatly. "If you behave all day, then

23

you may ride the carousel," Mama promised.

Benny started to whimper. "Why can't I go with *them?* I'm big enough."

Poor Benny, thought Rebecca. Life was a lot worse for her little brother than it was for her, even if he was a boy. She couldn't imagine having to stroll through a rose garden when the excitement of Steeplechase Park was beckoning.

"Promise me you'll stay together," Mama said, and the young people murmured their agreement.

"Enjoy your walk through the gardens," Max said to Mama. "I'm taking Lily on the Steeplechase horses. And that's just the beginning!" Lily smiled demurely, but Rebecca saw a sparkle of anticipation in her eyes.

"I want to ride the Steeplechase horses, too," Rebecca said. "Will you come with me, Ana?"

Victor held the tickets close to his chest. "I'll decide what rides you can take," he announced, talking like a schoolteacher. "Some of them might be too dangerous for you."

Rebecca looked impatiently over Victor's shoulder. Max and Lily were already moving forward in the long line that led to the racecourse.

The wooden horses raced down a mechanical track, with two riders on each one. She couldn't spend a day at Coney Island without going on this ride. After all, this was Steeplechase Park!

"It's not dangerous at all," Rebecca argued. "Give us our tickets."

"Let them go," Josef said. "As for me, I am setting my heart on roller coaster. That is much faster than wooden horses." He turned to Michael. "What you say, brother? Shall we wait for a *real* ride?"

Rebecca snatched two tickets from Victor and headed for the line with Ana. "We'll wait for you at the end of the ride!" Victor shouted, but Rebecca barcly listened as she and Ana hurried to the Steeplechase.

A small man dressed in the colorful silks of a horse jockey helped the girls onto a wooden horse, and Rebecca felt a shiver of anticipation. She looked down the racecourse. "I wonder how fast we'll go," she said, putting her arms around Ana's waist.

"Like the wind!" Ana grinned. "We will beat you," she called to Max as he and Lily climbed onto their horse. Lily sat at the front, with Max hugging her waist so she wouldn't fall. The jockey blew a bugle blast, and the wooden horses lunged down the track. Ana and Rebecca screamed with delight.

The wind tugged at Rebecca's hat and ruffled her hair as the horse picked up speed. With a lurch in her stomach, she felt the horse plunge down a steep slope. It sped around curves, up and down hills, and over a stream until it came to rest. The ride hadn't taken long, but Rebecca felt as if time had stopped. Riding a real racehorse couldn't be more thrilling than what she had just done.

The girls tripped down a ramp and across a brightly lit stage. A tiny clown cavorted around them, making silly faces. The girls laughed nervously as they exited past a huge statue of a pink and green elephant.

"Over here!" Victor called. Rebecca peered toward the dim area below the stage and saw the others seated in a row. The air crackled with excitement as hundreds of people eagerly watched the lit platform. Rebecca and Ana crowded in and sat down.

Sophie put her finger against her lips. "Wait until you see what's happening up there," she whispered, pointing up at the stage. "You were lucky you didn't get caught."

Before Rebecca had a chance to ask what Sophie meant, Max and Lily strolled across the stage, headed for the exit. The audience began to titter. Just as Lily reached the huge elephant, a gust of air blew up through the floor, blowing her dress high above her knees. Men in the audience whistled.

Lily fell against Max in a swoon, the back of her hand held limply to her forehead. The audience gasped, but Rebecca was sure Lily was just acting. She had practiced scenes like this before. Max supported Lily with one hand and awkwardly pushed down at her skirt with the other.

Just as Lily regained her composure and hurried to leave, the floor dipped. She struggled to regain her balance, clinging to Max for support, when another blast of air whipped up her skirt. The clown ran up on his short legs and gave Max a playful whack with a paddle. Max puffed out his chest and set his fists in a fighting pose. The crowd cheered. Lily held her clasped hands under her chin, batting her eyelashes and admiring her hero.

Max chased the clown around the stage. Then he scooped Lily up in his arms and carried her off the stage. The audience went wild, cheering and applauding.

"No one can get the better of Max," Rebecca crowed. "Especially not when there's an audience in front of him!" She pushed out of the row with Ana and the others as an expectant hush settled over the remaining crowd. Another unsuspecting couple was just coming across the stage toward the exit.

Sophie pushed her hands against her skirt. "I'm glad *I* didn't go on the Steeplechase horses," she confessed. "I would die of embarrassment if my skirt blew up like that."

"You can't be embarrassed at Coney Island," Lily laughed. "Oh, you might feel a bit foolish for a minute, but it's all in fun."

"That's why everyone loves to come here," Max added. "You can do things at Coney Island that you would never do at home, because all the rules are turned upside down." Max wiggled his eyebrows. "And now we're off to the Tickle Ride," he grinned. Lily laughed gaily as he whisked her away.

THRILLS, CHILLS, AND SKILLS

"I see this wheel from every spot," Ana said, pointing toward the gigantic Ferris wheel that turned slowly above them. "I'm dreaming of seeing the park and the ocean from up in the sky, just like a bird. But I'm afraid it will make me seasick, like the boat to America."

"The Ferris wheel is a sissy ride," Victor said. "Even Benny could go on it."

"That's not very nice," Rebecca said. "I think it looks kind of scary. I'll bet it's the highest ride in the whole park."

"Ana is a girl afraid of everything," said Michael.

"What if I hold your hand the whole time?" Victor teased.

"I'm not afraid of going up in the Ferris wheel," Rebecca said. "I'll go with her."

Victor shrugged and led the group to the Ferris wheel. With the attached strings, he tied one ticket onto a button on Ana's dress and another onto Rebecca's sash. "I don't want you losing these," he said. "After all, Papa did put me in charge."

As the girls moved up in line, Ana's sweaty hand gripped Rebecca's. The Ferris wheel towered above them, as tall as a skyscraper. When an empty car stopped in front of them, Ana hung back. "I think I am changing my mind," she said.

"We can't leave now," Rebecca protested, gently nudging her cousin into the swaying car. "Victor and Michael would tease us for the rest of our lives."

Inside the car, large windows covered with wire went around the top half of the cabin, providing a sweeping view in every direction. Rebecca held Ana's hand as more people entered the car. With each footstep, the car swayed. Ana's knuckles turned white as an attendant slid the door shut. Gears cranked and the car lurched up awkwardly, stopping and swinging as the next car was filled.

Several times, the car jolted higher, then halted and swayed.

"I am afraid," Ana whimpered. "Let me go off before I fall out!"

"We can't fall out," Rebecca assured her cousin. "Besides, it's too late to get off. But look, Ana, we're really moving now. No more stopping."

With one graceful movement, the car soared up into the sky and circled lazily over the park. Rebecca felt a feathery, floaty feeling in her stomach. "This must be what it's like to be a seagull," she marveled. "We're flying!"

31

Ana began to relax and gazed down to the park below. "Ooh!" she squealed. "People down there are like teensy ants. We are biggest people at Coney Island." Rebecca smiled with relief. Ana wasn't going to panic.

When the cars unloaded, Ana looked a bit queasy. She was the first one off when the cabin door opened. "Is wonderful, except for starting and stopping," she told the others when they were back on the ground. "I think I should go one more time, to prove to myself I am not afraid anymore."

Victor shook his head. "We can't always wait around for you two to get off a ride. There's lots more to do, without doing some rides twice." He untied their tickets and shoved them into his pocket as Rebecca seethed with annoyance.

Victor led everyone down an aisle filled with games of skill. A crash of broken glass startled them, and they turned to see what had happened. Nearby, a long line of people waited at a booth with glasses and dishes stacked up on the counter. A sign overhead said, "If you can't break up your own home, break up ours!" A young man threw a thick goblet, and a pile of dishes toppled to the ground, smashing to smithereens.

"Whatever are they doing?" Sophie gasped. A girl no older than Rebecca shrieked with horrified delight as she shattered an entire row of china plates. The crowd cheered as the barker awarded her a paper fan.

Rebecca blinked in astonishment. At home, everyone was careful not to break a dish, which would be expensive to replace. But at Coney Island, people happily paid to break them!

They moved on, past shooting galleries with rifles aimed at mechanical ducks, and tossing games of all kinds. Wonderful prizes lined the top shelf in each booth, and Rebecca thought it must be swell to go home with one. Suddenly, a row of Kewpie dolls caught her eye.

"Oh," she cried, pointing to the pot-bellied dolls. "Just look at those impish eyes and that cute tuft of hair. Remember those Kewpies on the cover of my school notebook?" she asked Ana. "I just adore Kewpies."

"Step right up, little lady," cried the barker. "All these little babies want is a good home. For one nickel, you can't lose." He turned to a pyramid of wooden pins set up behind him. "Just knock over these pins with a baseball and you can choose your prize. Everybody's a winner!"

Rebecca hesitated. She didn't have much money, and the game cost five cents. "Where in the world could you get your very own Kewpie for just one buffalo nickel?" asked the barker. Rebecca knew she couldn't buy one for twice as much. Lined up beside the dolls were baseball gloves, boxed cigars, and plush teddy bears. She would definitely choose a Kewpie.

"You could never win this game," Victor scoffed. "You couldn't hit the side of a tenement house with a baseball." A group of boys standing around the booth began to laugh. Rebecca felt her anger rising.

The barker glanced at the boys. "At Coney Island, everyone gets to do something new," he declared. "And you have three tries. Give it a whirl, little lady, and the Kewpie's yours."

"Let's go," Victor said. "We're wasting time."

"You think that only boys can throw?" Rebecca demanded. "What about hopscotch? You need good aim for that. Girls can throw—and aim, too."

"What about hopscotch?" mimicked one of the boys standing nearby.

"Hopscotch?" his friends echoed. They doubled over with laughter, slapping each other on the back.

They'll stop laughing if I win, thought Rebecca. With three chances, she was sure she could do it. She gave Ana her hat to hold, and then pulled a knotted handkerchief from her sash and counted out five pennies. She plunked them on the counter.

The barker set three balls on the counter. "Go to it, sweetheart."

Rebecca picked up the first ball. She eyed the stacked pins carefully, took aim, and threw with all her might. The ball whacked into the backboard without even grazing the pins. *I can do it,* she thought, steadying her nerves. *I have two more tries.*

Rebecca picked up the second ball and felt its weight. Maybe she didn't need to throw as hard as she had thought. She took a step back and threw a gentle toss. The pin at the very top of the pyramid wobbled, but stayed where it was.

"You call that throwing?" one of the boys jeered. He turned to his friends. "She throws just like a girl!"

"She *is* a girl," retorted another, and they all whooped with laughter.

Rebecca's heart was beating out of her chest.

The top rows tumbled down with a thunderous crash,
and Rebecca thought she had done it.

It throbbed high into her throat and up to her ears. Her face felt hot. She picked up the last ball, and no one made a sound. This time she used her whole arm, the way she had seen Victor pitch. The ball hit the pins. The top rows tumbled down with a thunderous crash, and the twins gasped. Rebecca thought she had done it—but two pins in the bottom row were left standing.

"Good try," consoled the barker. "And no one leaves without a prize." He handed her a small metal pin with a grinning Funny Face on it. The face that had looked so amusing when she arrived at Steeplechase now seemed to be mocking her. "Now that you've got the hang of it," the barker said, "why not try again? This time you're sure to win that Kewpie."

Lily had said that everyone felt foolish at Coney Island, and it was all in fun. But Rebecca felt completely humiliated, and it didn't seem fun or funny.

"You wasted five whole cents," Victor pointed out. "You should have listened to me."

"Leave me alone!" Rebecca blurted out. Tears welled in her eyes, and she turned away.

"Aww, don't take it so hard," Victor said. "I'm sorry I teased you. It's just that you don't have any practice throwing a baseball."

"Sure," Rebecca said. "Only *boys* can play baseball, right? Girls can't do anything!" A few people turned and stared. They were grinning as wide as the Funny Face, and Rebecca thought they looked horrid.

"I'm leaving," she said. "I'll meet you by the carousel later."

"You can't go off alone," Sadie said. "We promised to stay together."

"And I've got the tickets!" Victor reminded her, but Rebecca didn't care.

Ana caught her arm. "I'll go with you," she offered. "Then we won't really be breaking our promise, because *we'll* be together."

As the girls started to walk away, Rebecca heard the barker calling out, "Here you go, hot shot, give it a try. You can't lose!" Rebecca glanced back and saw Victor pick up a ball. Then she heard wooden pins crashing and cheers from the boys hanging around the booth. Victor must have won with just one throw.

STRIKING OUT ALONE

"How much money do you have?" Rebecca asked Ana. "We should be able to take a few more rides, even without the tickets."

Ana blinked. "I have no money," she said. "Papa doesn't have extra pennies for allowance."

Rebecca felt terrible. She never should have expected Ana to have pocket money. Ana had stayed with her out of loyalty, and she couldn't spoil her cousin's holiday.

"Let's see," Rebecca said, counting the change in her handkerchief. "I've still got ten cents. That's enough for each of us to choose one more ride, or we could get ice cream sodas instead."

Ana looked longingly at the Ferris wheel. "I would love to go up in the sky once more. Ice cream we can get at home, but I might never be at Coney Island again."

Ana was right about the ice cream. But without the tickets, she could do only one more amusement, and Rebecca wanted to try something different. "How about the fun house? Victor said it's a maze of crazy mirrors and we might never find our way out. But he can't stop us now." She handed her cousin a nickel and kept five pennies.

Ana looked doubtfully at the fun house entrance. "I guess so . . ." Her voice trailed off.

Rebecca thought for a moment. "Maybe I could go through the fun house while you ride the Ferris wheel. Do you think you could go alone?"

Ana lifted her chin. "I'm not afraid of going up anymore."

"I don't see why we can't do separate things," Rebecca said with a shrug. "How could it matter if we each do just one different amusement and then meet up again?"

Ana looked over her shoulder at the Ferris wheel, turning slowly above the noise and din of the park, and she nodded eagerly.

"Good," Rebecca said, pleased with her plan. She pointed to an empty bench outside the fun house. "After your ride, we'll meet back here at that bench." Ana nodded again and strode toward the Ferris wheel.

Rebecca paid her five cents and giggled her way through the darkened maze. She bumped into black walls that looked like open doorways, and followed long passageways that led her in circles. Crazy mirrors showed silly reflections. In one, she had a long head and a neck like a giraffe. In another, she was as short and fat as a pickle barrel. She stumbled across rippling floorboards, trying to make her way through the puzzle of criss-crossing corridors. At last, she stepped out into the sunshine, relieved and delighted.

Rebecca plopped down on the wooden bench to wait for Ana. Just as she leaned back, it suddenly buckled and folded up, and she went sprawling onto the sidewalk. A wave of laughter rose up from a group of bystanders.

What a mean trick! she thought. All those people

were just waiting for her to fall off so that they could laugh at her. She stood up and brushed sand from her hands and dress. She was about to stalk away when she thought about what Max would do. He'd never leave an audience without giving a performance.

Rebecca limped back to the bench, imagining that movie cameras were rolling behind her. She gingerly touched the seat back, and in a few seconds the bench folded and tilted down. Rebecca leapt into the air, jumping back in feigned fright. The crowd howled with laughter, and more people stopped to watch.

Exaggerating every movement, Rebecca walked warily around the bench, stroking it with her hand as if soothing an angry dog. Cautiously, she leaned her elbow against the back. The bench held for a moment, and she grinned with her victory, but then it collapsed, leaving her elbow poised in mid-air. Rebecca did a little pantomime, pretending she was comfortable leaning on nothing. She lowered her bent arm just a bit, and then again, searching for the bench. The audience, which had grown larger, erupted in a boisterous round of applause.

*Rebecca did a little pantomime, pretending she
was comfortable leaning on nothing.*

Rebecca was basking in the attention when the sound of fire horns and clanging bells cut through the air. The crowd drifted away to see what new excitement was unfolding in the park.

Shading her eyes, Rebecca looked around for Ana. Perhaps the line for the Ferris wheel was a long one. But Rebecca had been in the fun house quite a while, and she had performed her bench act after that. Maybe Ana had gotten lost. The horns blared louder and seemed to be drawing closer. Was this just more Coney Island noise, or was something wrong? She knew there had been huge fires at Coney Island in the past. Maybe another dangerous fire was sweeping through the park!

"What's going on?" Rebecca called as knots of people rushed past.

"It's the Ferris wheel," a woman said. "It's broken down."

Rebecca felt a wave of panic. She ran toward the Ferris wheel, pushing through the swelling crowd gawking at the huge ride. The horns and bells fell silent, and Rebecca heard people screaming from the swaying cars. They were screams of fear, not joy.

The riders in the lowest cars had already been

44

rescued, and two burly men cranked a thick handle
at the base of the Ferris wheel to bring the next car
down. Sweat glistened on their faces. Slowly,
another car was lowered and the frightened
passengers helped out to safety. Again, the men
began cranking. Suddenly Rebecca heard a loud
metal clank. The handle had stuck fast. The men
stood by helplessly, uncertain how to fix the newest
problem.

A fire truck rolled up. Four
firemen jumped out and began
ratcheting up the ladder. One section after another
rose toward the Ferris wheel cars. Higher and higher
the ladder reached, stopping just short of the lowest
swaying car. The crowd let out a collective gasp as a
fireman climbed to the top of the ladder and slid
open the cabin door.

Was Ana in that one? She would be in a terrible
panic. The cars rocked back and forth—the part of
the ride Ana had feared most. *Why did I leave her?*
Rebecca thought. *What will I tell Aunt Fannie and
Uncle Jacob?*

Rebecca craned her neck and shielded her eyes
from the glaring sun, straining to see. Her heart

pounded as one passenger and then another was slowly rescued down the ladder. Many were crying as they descended. Those still trapped in other cars shouted for help. Which car was Ana in?

For what seemed like hours, each car was emptied of its riders until only one full car remained. The crowd held its breath as the fireman reached out to the last trapped passenger. In the distance, Rebecca barely made out the figure of a small girl, frozen at the open door.

CHAPTER
FIVE
REACHING
NEW HEIGHTS

The crowd grew, and suddenly Rebecca caught sight of Benny, sitting on Papa's shoulders so that he wouldn't be crushed by the throng. She shrank back, trying to hide. But when she saw the worried looks on her family's faces, she waved her hand and called weakly, "Papa, over here!"

"The Ferris wheel's stuck," Benny chirped from his perch.

Mama hugged Rebecca tightly. "Thank goodness you're safe," she cried. "I was afraid you were trapped up there."

"Where are the other children?" Grandpa demanded. "Why you are alone?" But Rebecca didn't have a chance to answer before everyone was firing questions at her.

"Where are Ana and boys?" Aunt Fannie asked. Her voice quivered.

"Were you on the Ferris wheel?" Papa asked.

"Well, I *was* . . ." Rebecca began, ". . . before." Six pairs of worried eyes stared at her. Silence followed, and Rebecca dreaded what had to come next.

Max and Lily found them huddled in a group, and then Victor, Michael, and Josef shoved through the mob, with the twins on their heels.

"What's going on?" Victor asked. He looked at Papa with exasperation. "We *told* her not to leave."

Rebecca looked down at her shoes. "Ana's up there." The words were heavy on her tongue.

Uncle Jacob looked at the fire-truck ladder reaching toward the open door of the last car. Rebecca saw the flicker of recognition in his eyes. He turned to a policeman guarding a wooden barricade separating the crowd from the rescue operation.

"My daughter is in this car," he said, pointing. "I must go to her."

"Sorry, pal," the officer said. "You need training

to climb that ladder. It ain't as easy as it looks. Just relax—the fire crew will bring her down."

"She is afraid. Let me go," Uncle Jacob pleaded.

They watched anxiously as a fireman scaled the ladder and extended his hand toward Ana. She remained frozen in place, just out of reach. After a few minutes, the fireman came down alone. The crowd groaned.

Rebecca stepped up to the policeman, undaunted by his blue uniform and gleaming badge. "My uncle's right," she said. "Ana is petrified of the swaying car. She's never going to let a stranger pull her onto a wobbly ladder. Maybe if she sees a familiar face . . ." She tugged at his sleeve. "Please, sir, I can help her."

The policeman let out a barking laugh. "We've already got one little lady who's afraid of heights. We don't need two, now, do we?"

Papa spoke up. "Her father is a carpenter," he explained. "He's used to ladders and heights."

Mama tried to convince the policeman to let Uncle Jacob climb up, and Bubbie shook a finger at him and argued in Yiddish. Even the onlookers became fired up, shouting out their opinions to be heard above the hubbub and commotion.

Rebecca realized she'd never get permission to climb up to Ana, but somebody had to get up there—and soon. She shivered at the thought of her cousin stuck all alone in the swaying car. Without wasting another minute, Rebecca slipped under the barricade and inched toward the fire truck, hunching down so that she wouldn't be noticed.

"I can't get that kid to budge," reported the fireman, scratching his head under his cap. "She won't say a word, and I can't convince her that she won't fall if I hold on to her."

"What are you gonna do?" a second fireman asked.

"I'll try once more, and if she won't come down on her own, I'll have to make a grab for her and carry her down over my shoulder," the first one said. "She ain't gonna like it much, but I don't see what choice I have."

"That's a risky move when you're so high up," said his partner. "And it's not gonna help if she panics."

I can't let the fireman snatch Ana when she's already petrified with fear, Rebecca thought. She darted behind the uniformed men and crept along next to the fire truck. Firemen stood with their backs to her, craning their necks toward the teetering car.

Rebecca climbed onto the running board and made her way to the back of the truck. She gazed up at the ladder, which wobbled unsteadily. Afraid to think too long about what she was doing, Rebecca began to climb. As her feet reached for each rung, she tried not to look at the wide, empty gap between the steps.

The ladder bobbled, and Rebecca felt a fluttering in her stomach that was much stronger than when she had ridden on the Ferris wheel and held none of the pleasure. The ground receded farther and farther, the crowd below shrinking smaller and smaller. The deafening din of the park seemed muffled and distant.

As Rebecca climbed, she could see her cousin cringing, her face pale. "I'm coming, Ana," Rebecca called. "Don't be afraid." The sea breeze grew stronger as she climbed. One wayward gust caught Rebecca's straw hat and lifted it from her head. She watched helplessly as it sailed through the air toward the mob of people far, far below. Looking down made her head swim, and she quickly fixed

"I'm coming, Ana," Rebecca called. "Don't be afraid."

her eyes back on Ana. She moved more slowly, gripping the ladder tightly and making certain that each footstep landed squarely on the next rung. She didn't want to follow her hat, sailing down to the onlookers below.

At last, Rebecca approached the tip of the bobbing ladder. It wobbled up and down, while the Ferris wheel car in front of her swayed from side to side. A queasy feeling roiled her stomach.

"Come on, Ana," she coaxed. "Let's get down from here." But Ana didn't even seem to hear her.

"Come, *bubeleh*," she cooed, repeating one of her grandmother's favorite endearments. Maybe the sound of Yiddish would get through to Ana.

Her cousin blinked. "Rebecca!" she breathed hoarsely. "I can't get down."

Rebecca reached out, and Ana's trembling hand met hers. It was cold and clammy.

"Everyone's waiting for us," Rebecca said with a brightness she didn't feel. "We'll go get a cool drink. Wouldn't you like that?" Ana didn't move, but Rebecca could tell she was listening. "Turn around, and climb down backward. I'll hold on to you and guide you onto the ladder." Ana seemed to be considering the suggestion.

"Climbing this ladder is the best amusement in all of Steeplechase Park!" Rebecca went on. "Just think, the boys are going to be *so* jealous of us."

Ana let go of Rebecca's hand and slowly turned around. Planting her own feet carefully and holding on with one hand, Rebecca extended an arm toward her cousin. As she did so, a sinewy hand reached up and gripped Rebecca's waist. Startled, she glanced behind her and saw a husky fireman standing one rung below. In her concentration on Ana, she hadn't noticed him at all. Relief flooded through her, but she kept up her banter to keep Ana calm.

"The first step is the best," Rebecca said. "After that it gets *too* easy. Even Benny could do it."

Gingerly, Ana set her foot down, and Rebecca guided it onto the rung. Then Ana placed her other foot on the ladder. Rebecca held on to Ana's waist firmly, and with a squeaky yelp, Ana released her hold on the swaying car. Back down the ladder they went, one slow step at a time. Rebecca steadied Ana, and the fireman held on to Rebecca.

A roar went up from the gathering below as Rebecca and Ana were lifted off the truck onto solid ground. The entire family rushed to embrace them. Tears ran down Aunt Fannie's cheeks as she enfolded Ana in her arms.

Bubbie fanned herself furiously with a paper fan emblazoned with a grinning Funny Face. "So dangerous," she kept repeating. She looked around and complained to anyone who would listen, "This Coney Island, it's meshugah!"

Benny hugged Rebecca's knees. It was just the way he had hugged Victor after the Bar Mitzvah service, Rebecca thought. That seemed like weeks ago instead of just yesterday.

"Take *me* up the ladder, too!" Benny crowed. "I wanna climb up to the tippety top!"

A policeman stepped up and handed Rebecca her flyaway hat. "Saints preserve us, I wouldn't have believed it if I hadn't seen it with me own two eyes," he said. "One little lass rescuing another."

Rebecca turned gratefully to the fireman who had helped them down. She shook his hand and felt her own disappear into his massive palm.

"We've got to catch our breath," Papa said. "Let's go to Feltman's Restaurant for a cold glass of lemonade."

"I think I need something a little stronger than lemonade," Max chuckled. "You girls gave us quite a scare."

Lily held on to Max's arm as they walked, not realizing her scarf had fallen in limp folds across her shoulders. Everyone who looked in her direction seemed startled by her short hairdo. Bubbie's eyes widened for a moment, and Rebecca held her breath. But Bubbie simply looked heavenward without uttering one word of reproach.

"Look!" Benny cried, pointing at a carousel of carved horses gleaming with colorful jeweled trappings. "Those horses have real tails!"

The family walked past Feltman's dazzling carousel and settled at a large outdoor table. Benny tugged at Mama's dress. "I didn't get to ride on the carousel," he wailed. "And I was good all day."

"I think we've had enough rides," Mama said, talking over the vibrant organ music of the carousel.

Benny slumped forlornly in his chair. "No fair!" he complained.

"Did you hear about the daring rescue?" asked the waitress after Papa ordered their drinks.

"First-hand, I'm afraid," Papa replied. He pointed to Rebecca and Ana. "I watched the whole thing. You see, it was my daughter who rescued my niece."

"Heavens to Betsy!" exclaimed the waitress. She turned to Rebecca and Ana. "You two are the talk of Coney Island—and here you are right at my table!"

The waitress returned in a few moments with a tray of glasses and a large pitcher of icy lemonade. "Mr. Feltman says this is on the house," she announced grandly. "It's not every day we have a hero in our restaurant—or should I say, a *heroine*." Then she dropped a string of tickets onto the tray. "And these are for the carousel. Mr. Feltman wants you all to have a ride."

Benny jumped up, nearly toppling his chair. "I'm going to pick the biggest horse!"

When the waitress left, Papa fixed his gaze on Rebecca and Victor. "Mama and I told you children to stay together."

Rebecca hung her head. "I'm sorry, Papa. I really am."

Ana reached for Rebecca's hand, and Rebecca could feel that her cousin was still trembling. "It wasn't only Rebecca's fault," Ana said softly. "I wanted to ride on Ferris wheel one more time. We both broke our promise." She looked up, her bottom lip quivering slightly.

"You both made a serious mistake by going off alone," he said. Giving Rebecca a stern look, Papa slapped the table for emphasis. "Leaving the others was bad enough, but climbing up the ladder was terribly dangerous."

"But Papa," she protested, "I was sure that I could rescue Ana. How could that be wrong?"

Papa's expression softened, and Rebecca thought perhaps she saw a glimmer of pride in his eyes. He hesitated before he finally spoke. "You shouldn't disobey a police officer or put yourself in danger. Still, you did get Ana down, and thank goodness you're both safe now."

Lily nodded, her expression serious. "Sometimes we have to do what we think is right," she said quietly, "even if we don't do what's expected of us."

Rebecca felt confused. "How will I know when it's one of those times?"

Her question hung in the air for a moment. "I guess figuring that out is part of growing up,"

Papa said finally. He looked at the young people, and then let his gaze rest on Rebecca. "And you are growing up faster than I ever imagined."

"I'm growing up, too," Benny said. "So can I ride the carousel all by myself?"

"Maybe if you take Ana and Rebecca with you—and keep a close eye on them," Mama said with a smile.

Ana gave Rebecca's hand a light squeeze. "We are just like sisters," she whispered to Rebecca, "together in everything." Rebecca squeezed back.

Max raised his glass. "Here's to Rebecca," he toasted, "who rose above the crowd today."

"She and Ana reached new heights," Lily chimed in, clinking her glass against Max's. "People say anything can happen at Coney Island, and I guess it does!"

"I'll have to agree with that," Mama said. "I never thought I'd see Grandpa playing a carnival game."

Rebecca turned to Grandpa in surprise. "You played a game?"

"Dishes game," Grandpa replied with a sparkle in his eye. "Pay your nickel and break the dishes!"

"*Oy!* Such a clatter!" Bubbie exclaimed. "Real china, crashing and breaking all over. Such a mess like you've never seen!"

Grandpa gave Bubbie a tender pinch on her cheek. "You liked it, too," he chuckled.

"Bubbie!" squealed Sadie and Sophie in amazement. "You broke *dishes*?"

Bubbie shrugged and sipped her drink with a mysterious smile. "How you think I won this fan?" She nudged Grandpa with the folded fan. "This Mr. Feltman, he wants us to ride his carousel. It's meshugah, but maybe just a *little* ride, to make Mr. Feltman happy."

Rebecca, Ana, and the twins began to giggle. Were Bubbie and Grandpa really going to ride the carousel? Everything *did* seem topsy-turvy at Coney Island!

Victor held up a baseball glove. "Look, Pop, I won this at a throwing game with just one try. Isn't it a beaut?"

Rebecca's smile faded and she stiffened, remembering how she had lost after three tries. "I'd like to know why only boys play baseball, and not girls," she demanded.

"Actually, with a little practice, you could be a decent pitcher," Victor said generously.

"Hmph," Rebecca said. "Well, if I ever do win that throwing game, I sure won't pick a stupid baseball glove." She slurped her drink noisily.

Victor shrugged. "The game was so easy, I played twice," he said. "And I won the second time, too."

Rebecca groaned. "I suppose you took the box of cigars then," she said sarcastically. "After all, now you're a *man*, aren't you?"

Victor gave her a sheepish smile. "Look, I'm sorry I teased you back there," he said. "That was just a game. But when you climbed that ladder—that was really something."

At this rare praise from her brother, Rebecca felt all her anger drain out of her. "You deserved the glove," she admitted. Then she blurted out something she had been holding back. "You did a good job with your reading yesterday." She swallowed hard. "I was proud of you."

"What's this?" Papa said. "Victor and Rebecca are paying each other compliments? So it's true—anything *can* happen at Coney Island!"

61

Josef elbowed Victor. "Go on," he murmured.

"Show her," Michael urged.

With a mischievous grin, Victor slowly pulled a Kewpie doll from his pocket and handed it to Rebecca.

"You won this for me?" she asked. Rebecca hugged the doll close. Then she did something she hadn't done in a long time—she hugged her brother, too.

LOOKING BACK

AMERICA OUTDOORS
IN
1914

Seaside fun at New York City's Rockaway Beach

In most parts of America, summertime in the city is hot and humid. In the days before air conditioning, city dwellers often found their small apartments stifling. Children could sometimes find shady parks to play in, and many children played and swam in New York City's rivers. But the best way to cool off was a trip to the seaside.

Some families rented a cottage by the sea for the summer. Others went just for the day, as Rebecca's family did.

In Rebecca's day, girls' swimwear covered most of the body.

Crowds Going On Excursion Boat For Coney Island, New York.

By 1914, with the development of cheap, fast travel by subway, trolley, and ferryboat, it was easier for families to make one-day trips to the beach and other outdoor destinations. As America's cities grew larger, seaside resorts grew bigger and more popular. In Rebecca's time, the biggest and most popular seaside resort of all was on a strip of shore-line in Brooklyn known as Coney Island.

Visitor's guide to Coney Island

Coney Island was like a circus, a carnival, and an amusement park all rolled into one. Besides the rides, games, and fun houses, you could see clowns, jugglers, acrobats, and even camels and elephants strolling through the exhibits. Steeplechase Park, where Rebecca went, was only one part of Coney Island. Another area, Luna Park, featured exotic locations,

Coney Island as it looked in 1903. By Rebecca's time, it was even bigger.

such as an Eskimo village complete with real Eskimos and sled dogs, and re-created spectacular disasters such as the volcanic eruption of Mount Vesuvius.

In 1914, most people couldn't travel to exotic places, and movies with special effects didn't exist, so sights like these were astonishing to behold. To children in Rebecca's time, Coney Island was every bit as thrilling as Disney World is to children today.

Unlike theater entertainment, where the audience simply sat and watched, at Coney Island people actively participated in the fun and adventure. When a bench collapsed under you or your dress flew up, you became part of the entertainment for everyone else! Coney Island appealed to children and adults alike because it allowed them to break the usual rules they lived by. In the early 1900s, America was just coming

These Victorian girls express the free, fun-loving spirit of Coney Island.

out of a time when there were lots of very strict rules for proper behavior, known as the *Victorian age*. Although most people didn't quite realize it yet, they were starting to grow tired of all the rules. So they loved going to Coney Island, where it was okay to act silly and crazy in public and to do things that you didn't do at home. As one man put it, "When you are at Coney, you cast aside your hampering reason and become a plain lunatic." At Coney Island, a girl like Rebecca might well decide to try a boy's skill, such as baseball throwing, and even dignified, respectable grandparents smashed plates and rode the carousel—things they would never have done in their everyday lives!

Grandmothers enjoying a Coney Island carousel ride in 1952, just as Bubbie does in the story

No trip to Coney Island was complete without eating at Feltman's Restaurant, which could serve 8,000 people at a time.

Coney Island also appealed to the public for another reason: it made people feel equal to one another. It didn't matter if you were rich or poor, young or old, a new immigrant or a long-time American. Everyone rode the same rides, played the same games, and took the same pratfalls as everyone else. Despite the strange, topsy-turvy surroundings, at Coney Island immigrant families like the Rubins felt like real Americans, having fun in an especially American way, just like everyone else.

Girls loved to send their friends postcards, like the three on this page, from Coney Island.

Glossary

Bar Mitzvah *(bar MITS-vah)*—In Hebrew, this translates as "son of the commandment." It refers to the ceremony honoring a boy's first reading of the Jewish Bible, and also to the boy himself.

bubbie *(BUH-bee)*—**Grandmother,** in Yiddish

bubeleh *(BUH-beh-leh)*—A Yiddish endearment, much like **dearest**

kosher *(KOH-sher)*—A Yiddish word meaning **fit to eat** under Jewish dietary laws

kvetching *(KVETCH-ing)*—The Yiddish word for **complaining**

mazel tov *(MAH-zl tof)*—Hebrew for **congratulations**

mensch *(mench)*—In Yiddish, an **honorable person**

meshugah *(meh-SHOO-gah)*—**Crazy,** in Yiddish and Hebrew

oy *(oy)*—A Yiddish exclamation, similar to **oh!**

Shabbos *(SHAH-bis)*—Yiddish for **Sabbath,** the day of rest

Torah *(TOR-uh)*—The first five books of **Jewish Scripture,** usually written on a scroll

A SNEAK PEEK AT

CHANGES FOR

*Rebecca and Ana decide to make a movie about
a factory worker and give it a happy ending.
But Ana won't play fair.*

"I f only my parents would go to a movie and enjoy themselves," said Ana, "instead of worrying all the time."

"What are they worried about?" Rebecca asked.

"Jobs and money," Ana answered. "Papa and Josef are not paid fairly at the coat factory. No one is. The workers are asking for better pay. If the bosses don't agree, the workers might go on strike. Then Papa and Josef won't earn any money at all."

"Then let's hope there won't be a strike," said Rebecca. She knew Ana's family earned barely enough to make ends meet. Without Uncle Jacob and Josef working, the family would be in serious trouble.

Ana looked so worried that Rebecca wanted to cheer her up. "I've got a great idea," she said. "Let's act out a movie about a worker in a coat factory. Movies have happy endings, so in ours everyone will get a raise."

Ana perked up. "That sounds good! And since I know what the factories are like, I could play the boss."

The girls bounded up the front stoop and into Ana's tenement building. Rebecca followed her

cousin up two flights of creaky wooden stairs. In the tiny run-down apartment, Aunt Fannie had cleaned everything to a shine, and Uncle Jacob had painted the kitchen walls a sunny yellow.

Ana took one of her father's hats from a nail on the wall and plopped it on her head. "I'll be Mr. Simon. He's the boss." She draped her mother's shawl around Rebecca's shoulders and sat her at a small table in the tiny parlor. "You can be a poor stitcher who's just come to America."

"Okay," Rebecca said. "I'm Katerina Kofsky, fresh off the boat at Ellis Island." Rebecca bent over the table as if she were leaning over a sewing machine. "*Whirrrrrr*," she murmured softly, pretending to guide fabric under a needle.

"You really have to slump over," Ana directed. "Look as if you're too tired and hot to even push the fabric through."

Rebecca followed Ana's instructions, imagining her shoulders ached from bending over the machine. She didn't need to imagine working in stifling heat, since Ana's apartment was so hot and stuffy, it didn't seem that a factory sweatshop could be any worse.

Ana strode back and forth. "Faster! Faster!" she ordered. "You're too slow."

Rebecca really was sweating. She reached up and wiped the perspiration from her forehead.

"Aha!" Ana shouted, pointing an accusing finger. "You are not allowed to stop your machine without my permission, Miss Kofsky!" Ana pretended to pull out a notebook and write in it. "You will lose one hour of pay this week."

Rebecca clasped her hands together. "Please, Mr. Simon," she begged, "I was only wiping off my forehead so I could see the work better. Don't take any money from my pay. If my family can't pay the rent, the landlord will throw us onto the street!"

"And no talking!" Ana gave a mean smile. "I will be kind to you, Miss Kofsky, and only take out a nickel for talking instead of working."

"Not *more* from my pay," Rebecca cried. She leaned over and pretended to sew again. "Oh, please, Mr. Simon. I am working hard."

"Still talking? That's another nickel! Soon you will learn to do what Simon says." Ana let out a nasty chuckle.

"What?" Rebecca was indignant. "How can you

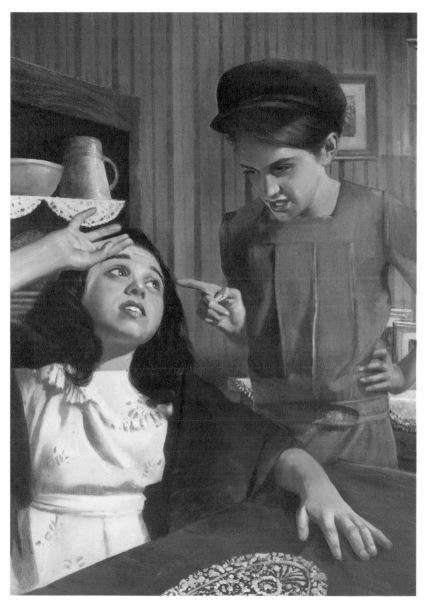

*"You are not allowed to stop your machine
without my permission, Miss Kofsky!"*

punish me for nothing? If you don't treat the workers fairly, we will walk out of this factory and go on strike. Then you'll be sorry."

Ana sneered. "Go ahead and strike. There are plenty more workers coming off the boat who will take this job in a minute." She pointed to the door. "You do what I tell you, or you're fired."

Rebecca's heart was beating fast. No matter what she said, Ana seemed to get the better of her. "Why are you being so mean, Ana?" she sputtered. "In our movie, the workers are supposed to get a raise. You're not playing fair!"

Ana folded her arms across her chest. "I'm not Ana—I'm Mr. Simon. That means I can do whatever I want, and you have to go along with it."

Anger rose in Rebecca's chest. She couldn't do anything without being punished. The movie wasn't fun anymore.

"CUT!" Rebecca yelled, so loudly that her cousin flinched. Rebecca pulled off the shawl. "Why are you doing this, Ana?"

"I'm acting in a movie, just like you said," Ana replied. "I'm being a factory boss."

"Well, you don't have to be so mean," Rebecca

protested. "And so unfair."

Ana shrugged. "Josef tells me lots of stories about the factory, and that's how the bosses are."

Just then the door opened. Ana's mother and her brother Michael entered the apartment.

"We went to an important workers' meeting," Michael told his sister. "People gave speeches about how to make the clothing shops better places to work. If the bosses don't change things, there's going to be a huge strike." His eyes shone with excitement.

Rebecca almost felt like cheering. If all the workers walked out together, that would show those bosses they couldn't get away with being so unfair! Then she remembered what Ana had said—the bosses could just hire new workers, and nothing would change. "Do you really think a strike would help?"

"It's the only thing left to do," Michael insisted. "Things can't get any worse than they are now."

"Yes, they can," Aunt Fannie said quietly. "If your papa and Josef can't bring home the pay every week, things will get a lot worse—for us."

READ ALL OF REBECCA'S STORIES,
available at bookstores and *americangirl.com.*

MEET REBECCA
When Rebecca finds a way to earn money,
she keeps it a secret from her family.

REBECCA AND ANA
Rebecca is going to sing for the whole school.
Will cousin Ana ruin her big moment?

CANDLELIGHT FOR REBECCA
Rebecca's family is Jewish.
Is it wrong for Rebecca to make a
Christmas decoration in school?

REBECCA AND THE MOVIES
At the movie studio with cousin Max,
Rebecca finds herself in front of the camera!

REBECCA TO THE RESCUE
A day at Coney Island brings more
excitement and thrills than Rebecca expected.

CHANGES FOR REBECCA
When Rebecca sees injustice around her, she
takes to the streets and speaks her mind.